P9-DDC-447

JACK and the BEANSTALK

FIRST EDITION

Library of Congress Cataloging-in-Publication Data

Howe, John, 1957–
Jack and the beanstalk/retold and illustrated by John Howe — 1st ed.
p. cm.
Summary: A boy climbs to the top of a giant beanstalk where he uses his quick wits to outsmart a giant and make his and his mother's fortune.
ISBN 0-316-37579-9
[1. Fairy tales. 2. Folklore — England 3. Giants — Folklore.]
I. Title.
PZ8.H837 Jac 1989
398.2'1'0941 — dc19
[E] 88-23034
CIP
AC

10 9 8 7 6 5 4 3 2 1

NIL

Published simultaneously in Canada
by Little, Brown & Company (Canada) Limited

Printed in Italy

Also by John Howe

RIP VAN WINKLE

For my son Dana James,
who has yet to meet his life's share of
giants and beanstalks

JACK and the BEANSTALK

RETOLD AND ILLUSTRATED BY

JOHN HOWE

LITTLE, BROWN AND COMPANY
Boston Toronto London

Once upon a time there was a poor widow who lived with her son, Jack, in a small cottage. Jack was a lazy boy who did not like to work, so all they had to live on was the milk from their old cow. They sold the milk at the market and managed to eke out a meager living.

One morning the cow gave no milk, and the widow could see that she and Jack were in danger of starving.

"Jack," she said, "there is nothing for it but to sell our cow and use whatever we get for her to help us survive."

"Cheer up, Mother," Jack replied. "I'll go to the market and sell our cow for a good price. Never fear, all will be well."

So Jack set off for the market. On his way, he met an old man who offered him five brightly colored beans for the cow. At first, Jack refused such a small offer.

"It's a good trade," said the old man, "for these beans are magic and will bring you a great fortune."

"A fortune is just what I need," replied Jack, and he traded his cow then and there.

Jack returned home and, whistling happily, went through the door of the small cottage.

"Look, Mother, look at the wonderful magic beans I have traded for our cow," Jack said.

"Beans!" his mother cried. "Oh, Jack, there is no such thing as magic. You stupid boy! You have ruined us." And with that she took the beans and threw them out the window.

Seeing how upset his mother was, Jack told her he was sorry he had made such a poor bargain, and they both went to bed hungry that night.

When Jack woke the next morning, he hopped from his bed and went to the window to breathe the fresh air.

Imagine his surprise when he looked from his window and saw that the beans that his mother had thrown out the window had taken root and sprung up overnight into a huge beanstalk that rose up, up into the clouds!

Now, Jack was an adventurous lad, and while not good at trading, he was very good at climbing. He decided right away that he would discover where the beanstalk went. So he ran from his house, took hold of the great vine, and up, up into the sky he went.

At long last he reached the top and saw in front of him a long, broad road that led directly to a great stone castle.

Curious, Jack walked to the castle and there, at its portal, he met a very big woman with a very big porridge pot in her hand. Jack was hungry and, seeing the porridge pot, asked, "Please, lady, could you give me some breakfast?"

"You look like a good boy," said the woman, "and I would like some company. Come in and I will give you some bread and milk. But you must be careful, my lad. For if my husband, the giant, comes home and sees you, he'll eat you up in a second. There is nothing he likes better to eat than human flesh!"

These words frightened Jack, but he was very hungry, so he entered the castle.

Jack had just finished his meal when the castle began to tremble and shake: *thump! thump! thump!* The giant was approaching.

"Quick," cried the giant's wife, "hide here." And she popped Jack into the unlit oven just as the giant came in.

"Wife," the giant rumbled, "what is it I smell?

"Fe Fi Fo Fum
I smell the blood of an Englishman.
Be he alive or be he dead
I'll grind his bones to make my bread."

"Nonsense," his wife replied. "You must smell the stew I've cooked for you. There is no one here. Come, sit and eat."

The giant believed his wife, so he sat and ate the stew in great mouthfuls. When he was finished, he called out, "Bring me my hen."

The giant's wife brought him a plump hen, and the giant commanded, "Lay!"

As Jack peeped out from the oven, he saw the hen lay a golden egg. When the giant commanded, another golden egg appeared.

The giant amused himself with the hen for a long time, but eventually he became sleepy. His head rested on the table and his snores shook the castle walls.

When Jack saw that the giant was asleep, he crept from the oven, seized the hen, and ran out of the castle. He ran to the beanstalk and slithered down to safety.

"Look, Mother!" he cried as he showed her the hen. "The beanstalk really was magical!"

Jack and his mother lived for many months on the riches that the hen provided, but then Jack felt a great longing to climb the beanstalk once again. So one gray day, Jack climbed the mighty vine and presented himself at the giant's castle.

"Go away," said the giant's wife. "Aren't you the boy who came here before? My eyes are not what they once were, but I think I recognize you. My husband was furious at the loss of his hen, you know."

"Well, ma'am, if you let me in and feed me, I can tell you something about all of that," said Jack.

The giant's wife was curious about what Jack might say, so she let him in and gave him some bread and cheese.

Jack had scarcely tasted a mouthful of his food when — *thump! thump! thump!* — they heard the giant's footsteps. As quick as a wink Jack once again hid in the oven.

In came the giant and for the second time he bellowed,

"Fe Fi Fo Fum
I smell the blood of an Englishman.
Be he alive or be he dead
I'll grind his bones to make my bread."

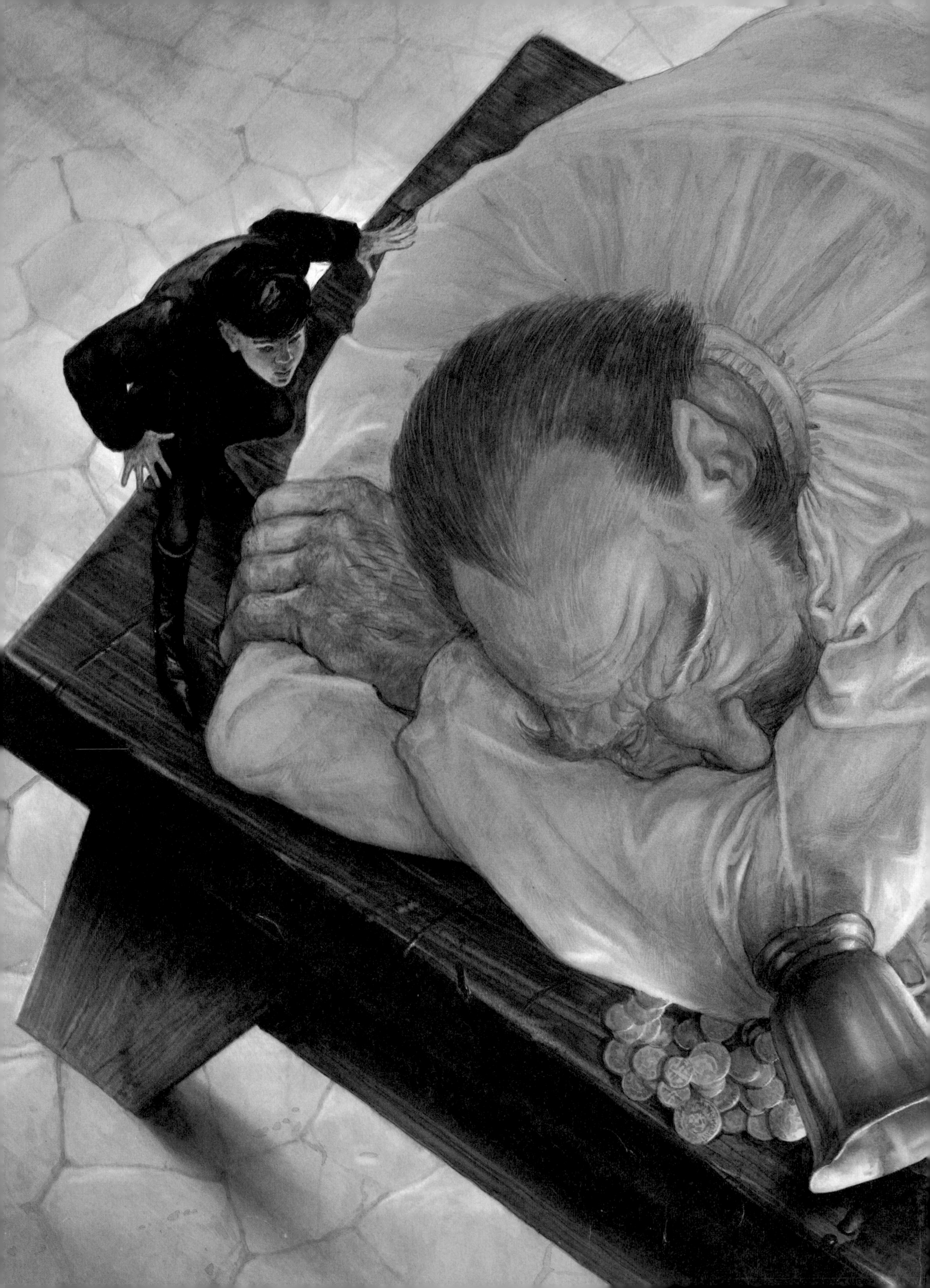

"Hush now, dear," said the giant's wife. "I believe what you smell are the three cows I've roasted as a snack for you. Come, sit and eat."

The giant did as he was bid, and after he had eaten every bit of every cow he said, "Bring me my gold."

His wife brought him three bags of gold and emptied one out on the table.

As Jack watched, the giant counted his gold pieces until his eyes shut, and, snoring mightily, he fell into a deep sleep.

As stealthily as a cat, Jack crept from the oven, seized a bag of gold, and staggered to the beanstalk. He dropped through the clouds like a stone through water, and he soon was home.

"Look, Mother, look!" he said as he showed the gold to the astonished woman. "The beanstalk has helped us once again."

For the next three years, Jack and his mother lived on the gold that he had taken from the giant's castle. At the end of that time, the coins were almost gone and Jack was anxious to visit the giant's castle once more.

After he had climbed the beanstalk, Jack wondered if the giant's wife would let him into the castle for a third time. Not wishing to press his luck, he hid outside the castle door until the woman came outside to hang out her wash. Just as the door was about to shut, Jack darted from his hiding place and scampered into the kitchen.

Jack hid in the oven once again and it was not long before the giant and his wife entered the kitchen.

"Wife, what is that smell?" demanded the giant.

"Fe Fi Fo Fum
I smell the blood of an—"

But before he could finish, his wife interrupted him. "Do not fret, my dear. No one is here. That rascal who stole your hen and your gold has not been seen for years. I do not smell anything. You must have a cold. Come, sit and eat."

The giant grumbled, but he did as he was bid. After he had eaten his fill, he ordered his wife to bring him his harp.

Jack crept from the oven and saw a truly beautiful harp on the table in front of the giant. Imagine Jack's astonishment when the giant commanded, "Play!" and the harp began to play and sing exquisite music without anyone touching it!

This beautiful music entranced the giant, quickly lulling him to sleep.

As soon as he thought it was safe, Jack slipped from the oven, seized the harp, and began to run toward the beanstalk.

But the harp sang out loudly, "Help me, master, I am being stolen away."

The giant, hearing the harp's cry of distress, shook his groggy head and then, seeing Jack, gave a great roar and jumped from the table.

"Come back, you villain," the giant thundered as he chased after Jack. "It was you who stole my hen and my gold. You will not steal my harp. I'll eat you up!"

Catching the harp to him, Jack reached the beanstalk and slid down quickly. He could hear the giant climbing slowly down after him.

"Quick, Mother, bring me an ax!" Jack called, as he saw the giant's foot break through the clouds. There was no time to spare. The giant was coming closer and closer. Jack took the ax and chopped and chopped. The beanstalk finally came crashing to the ground, bringing the giant with it. He was killed where he fell.

All ended well. The hen continued to lay golden eggs and the harp sang lovely songs for Jack and his mother. Jack grew up to be a gallant gentleman. He married a beautiful princess, never again thought about the magic beanstalk, and all lived happily ever after.